Casey

Dotty

Finch

Newt

Migs

Molene

Rokko

For Elizabeth Hodgkinson

First American edition published in 2014 by Andersen Press USA, an imprint of
Andersen Press Ltd.
www.andersenpressusa.com
First published in Great Britain in 2014 by Andersen Press Ltd.,
20 Vauxhall Bridge Road, London SW1V 2SA.
Published in Australia by Random House Australia Pty.,
Level 3, 100 Pacific Highway, North Sydney, NSW 2060.
Distributed in the United States and Canada by
Lerner Publishing Group, Inc.
241 First Avenue North
Minneapolis, MN 55401 USA
For reading levels and more information, look up this title at www.lernerbooks.com.
Color separated in Switzerland by Photolitho AG, Zürich.
Printed and bound in Malaysia by Tien Wah Press.
Library of Congress Cataloging-in-Publication data available.
ISBN: 978-1-4677-5014-1
eBook ISBN: 978-1-4677-5015-8
1 - TWP - 1/28/14

MIX
Paper from
responsible sources
FSC® C012700
FSC
www.fsc.org

TOYS

"Come on, Migs," calls out his Mum,
"Starting school's fantastic fun!

She hugs him tight, she waves goodbye.
Migs is trying not to cry.

He watches all the fun and sighs,
"I wish I wasn't quite so shy."

He finds a hat, a cape, some boots.

He feels so brave in this new suit.

"I'm **MIGHTY MIGS** and I declare

That I'm as **strong** as any **bear!**
I'm not a shy mouse any **more!**

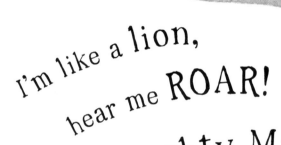

I'm like a lion,
hear me ROAR!

I'm Mighty Migs. Just look and see.

No train can move as fast as me!"

"Please, slow down, Migs!"

Miss Doodle calls.

"That cape's too long!

You'll trip and fall."

"Stop!" Rokko says. "It's not the same,
It looked so nice before you came."

Through tears he says, "Migs, go away!
I'd rather that you didn't stay."

Migs looks to find a place to hide,
He sees a box and climbs inside.

Migs sits and thinks. At last it's clear
"Miss Doodle, I've a **great idea!**"
Miss Doodle claps, "I'll call the team.
This plan's a **winner**, what a **scheme!**"

Soon everyone does what they can
To help Migs with his **super plan.**

"SSHH!" whispers Migs. "I'll take a look . . .
He's in the corner with a book."

They sound the fanfare, Rokko squeals,
"**My boat!** I can't believe it's real."
Migs says, "We made it just for you."
Says Rokko, "Look, there's room for two."

They take positions,

read the map.

Sail round the classroom . . .

then sail back.

At lunch there's tales of things they've seen.

That mermaid looked quite like Molene.

And Rokko's painted something new.
"Look, Migs," he says. "It's me and you."

The story's over, that's the end.

They wave goodbye to
their new friends.

Migs says, "Mum, if it's OK,
Can I go back there every day?"

Newt

Molene

Finch

Migs

Casey

Rokko

Dotty